W9-BVP-836

ALIEN IN MY POCKET

On Impact!

by
Nate Ball

illustrated by
Macky Pamintuan

HARPER

An Imprint of HarperCollinsPublishers

Alien in My Pocket: On Impact!
Text by Nate Ball, copyright © 2014 by HarperCollins Publishers
Illustrations by Macky Pamintuan, copyright © 2014 by HarperCollins Publishers
Library of Congress catalog card number: 2014935757
ISBN 978-0-06-231492-5 (trade bdg.) — ISBN 978-0-06-221629-8 (pbk.)
Typography by Sean Boggs
14 15 16 17 18 LP/RRDH 10 9 8 7 6 5 4 3 2 1
❖
First Edition

Contents

Late

My legs are spaghetti.

Or socks filled with pancake batter.

Or octopus tentacles.

Or wait: soggy wet beach towels.

That's it: my legs are soggy octopus tentacles in dress socks filled with spaghetti and pancake batter.

At least that's what it felt like as I rode my bike to school. I was exhausted.

And Amp was to blame for it all, of course.

He made me miss my bus . . . again! Third time in one week. That was a new record.

My dad drove me to school the first two times, but this time he had a big presentation at work.

So there I was, riding my bike as fast as I could to get to a spelling test that I hadn't studied for.

My life was a mess. Before my pesky blue alien crash-landed his crummy spaceship into my bedroom, I had a fairly regular life. I played baseball. I got decent grades. I slept eight to ten hours a night. Now I had Amp to worry about. It's like he travelled a bajillion miles through space and time just to get on my nerves. And oh, yeah, to scout Earth to see if it was worth invading.

My best friend, Olivia, is the only other person who knows about Amp, but she gets to go home at the end of the day.

Here's some friendly advice: never adopt an alien.

Trust me.

I leaned into the corner of Jacob Drive at full speed and my overly stuffed backpack almost sent me spilling to the pavement.

That's when I saw them up ahead in the middle of the street: a pack of hulking black crows standing around like a gang of misfits waiting to steal my lunch money.

Crows give me the creeps. I don't know why, but they make me uneasy. They are bad news . . . with wings.

5

I leaned over my handlebars, tapped into whatever strength remained in my watery legs, and rode right at them. They squawked and screeched and flew out of my way at the last possible second. "HA!" I shouted. "Out of the street, you turkeys!"

Seconds later, I roared toward the bike racks outside of Reed Elementary School. I felt like a knight returning from a successful battle, ready to give the king good news.

But my smile disappeared almost instantly.

My bike wasn't slowing down. I squeezed the brake levers on my handlebars. Nothing. I had no brakes! I was going full speed at the first bike rack!

One last thought shot through my brain before impact: THIS IS YOUR FAULT, AMP!

Lemon Head

At least I had gotten out of the spelling test.

I was now lying in my bed trying like crazy to find a silver lining.

I wasn't dead.

And the arm that now hung in a sling wasn't my throwing arm. (I'm a lefty, but I throw right-handed. Go figure.) If you're going to dislocate your shoulder, it's best not to destroy your baseball career at the same time.

The phone rang. I could hear my mom say hello to Coach Lopez. "Apparently, somebody stole his bike brakes," she explained to him. "I know—weird. But Zack wanted me to mention that it's his left arm. His throwing arm sustained no damage. He even wrote that down for me. How cute is that?"

"Mom!" I yelled down, and she stopped her conversation and said, "Yes, Zacky?" But I couldn't think of how to tell her that she wasn't supposed to tell him that she was reading my instructions without making matters worse! "Nothing." I sighed, and she went back to talking to Coach Lopez while I propped myself up in my bed.

My head was loopy from the pain pills. I felt mentally jumbled. My brain kept wandering off. My skull felt like it was filled with lemonade and goldfish.

But at least my shoulder didn't hurt too badly.

I wondered if my little bike rack incident would make the yearbook. That'd be so embarrassing, but also kind of cool if they gave my accident a whole page.

Luckily, classes were about to start when the ambulance finally arrived, but a decent-sized crowd had still hung around. I remember hearing the mix of different voices as I lay wedged between two bikes.

"Is he dead?" someone wondered.

"Who taught that idiot how to ride a bike?"

"Don't be mean—maybe he's blind."

"That's ridiculous, why would a blind kid ride a bike to school?"

"Who is it?"

"I think it's Shane Kerr."

"No, that's Debbie Finster," another kid corrected her. He sounded so sure. "Her dad is my dentist."

"Oh, yeah, that was Debbie for sure," a girl said sadly. I took particular interest in her use of the past tense.

Principal Luntz was the first adult on the scene. "I should have known it would be you, Zack McGee," was all he said. He shook his head at me with a frown, as if I had meant to pop my arm bone from its socket just to avoid a spelling quiz.

The ride in the back of an ambulance was pretty much what you'd expect: it smelled like medicine, you couldn't see where you were going, and they didn't play music. Apparently, a dislocated shoulder doesn't merit using the siren, which was a little disappointing.

Now here I was, in my bed, my baseball season ruined—and I had a combination lemonade stand and aquarium open for business in my head.

I hadn't seen the hamster-sized alien who'd made me late in the first place since I got home. He was probably hiding. Amp knew he'd get an earful when he came out. I didn't remember dozing off, but I must have.

I dreamed of crows chewing the brakes off my bike as I served them cups of cold lemonade poured directly from my nose.

Maybe we should start breaking those big white pain pills in half.

Late Again

The most annoying thing about living with an alien is the impact it has on your sleep.

Since Amp's crippled spaceship dented my bedroom wall, getting a good night's sleep had become about as likely as catching a one-eyed unicorn that burps rainbows and farts lightning.

On the planet Erde, there's no such thing as sleep. Amp doesn't understand why I need it. He ignores my complaints about being woken up all the time. It's like living with a misfiring cuckoo clock.

But thanks to the mind-bending pain pills, I actually had a full night's rest. Even a four-inch-tall alien on my chest couldn't wake me before I was ready.

"It's about time," Amp said in his strange,

15

high-pitched voice.

"Thanks for your concern about my arm," I said with a sigh.

"Yes, I see you have a boo-boo."

"A boo-boo? I almost died!"

"That device on your arm doesn't indicate a severe injury," he said, stroking his chin.

"Oh, thanks a lot, Doctor Amp," I said. "I have a rash I'd like you to take a look at when you're done."

"Whoa! Grumpy . . ."

"You're to blame for all this, you know."

"Me? What did I do?"

"You made me late for school."

"How exactly did I do that?"

"Let's start with the fact that your people are about to invade Earth. That doesn't help." I ran my fingers through my hair with the hand from my good arm. "Plus, somebody stole the brake cables on my bike. That's why I crashed."

I waited for sympathy, but Amp was silent. "What's wrong?" I asked. "You look gassy. Please don't fart right now. I'm not sure I can run away."

"You rode your bike?" he said in a faraway

voice. "You never ride your bike on school days."

"I know, but I missed the bus. Remember? I was helping you fix a switch on your lame rocket-ship."

"But I thought your father was going to drive you!"

"He already drove me twice this week. He said my lateness was a character flaw."

"You can't argue with that," Amp said quietly.

"Whatever. He had a big presentation and couldn't drive me, and Mom had already left for work."

Amp was now pacing in front of the alarm clock. I could see it was 11:30 a.m. Wow, that really was a good night's sleep!

"I should have told you."

"Told me what?"

"I borrowed those brake wires when you were at school on Monday."

"Why on Earth would you do that!?!" I shouted.

"As you know, my landing system didn't function when I arrived here, so I was trying to fix the braking flaps on my . . ." His voice trailed off when he saw the look on my face. He backed farther away from me. "Easy now, Zack." He looked nervous. "Remember, you have a boo-boo."

"I should have known it was you," I said between gritted teeth.

With a groan, I started to get up, but pain shot through my shoulder. He instantly disappeared from sight, using one of his alien mind-control abilities.

"Your Jedi tricks don't work on me anymore, Amp," I said. It was true; I had been teaching myself how to to deflect his invisible brain signals. At that instant, I saw him scamper across my bookshelf. "I SEE YOU!"

He sort of blinked on and off in my vision as I concentrated on blocking his mind trick. He dove off the bookshelf and ran across the carpet and into the closet.

"You better hide, you little blue headache."

Honestly, my arm hurt too much to actually chase him. It hurt just to swing my legs off my bed. I stared at the wall, my anger at Amp boiling.

Just then, there was a knock on my door

"Zack, it's time for your pill, and you have a visitor," Mom sang through the door.

I knew who the visitor was before the door opened.

"Come on in, Olivia," I groaned.

04

Olivia + Mike + Amp

I washed down my pain pill as Olivia swept into my room like she owned the place. That's how she is.

She had a stack of worksheets from school in one hand, a roll of SweeTarts for Amp in the other, and one of those clear plastic pet balls under her arm.

Inside the plastic ball was her new hamster, which she had named Mike, which must be the most inappropriate name for a hamster ever.

I had suggested a whole list of great names.

"How about Ace?" I had pleaded. "Or Skittles? Or PopTart? Or Yoda? Or Brownie? Buttercup? Fuzzface? Nibbles? Shaggy? Tinkerbell? Sparky? Monkey Butt? You can even name it Bubba. It's so cute I could puke!"

Olivia was having none of it. "No way," she'd said. "He's Mike."

She placed Mike in his ball onto the carpet. Mike instantly started rolling around, exploring my messy room. Olivia toed my open door shut so Mike wouldn't wind up bouncing down the stairs by accident.

She tossed the short stack of fluttering worksheets onto my desk. "Those are from the lovely Miss Martin," she said. She looked around and didn't see Amp, so she tossed the roll of Swee-Tarts on top of the worksheets.

"All those worksheets are from one day?" I croaked.

"Yesterday and today," she said matter-of-factly. "Today is Friday, Zackaroni. You missed Thursday altogether. You're piling up the makeup tests like crazy."

I groaned. "I almost died. You'd think Miss Martin would cut me some slack and let me miss a few tests. And what are you doing here? It's not even noon. Why aren't you in school?"

"I convinced Miss Martin I needed to come see you and bring you your work. Cheer you up. I

23

told her you needed a lot of cheering up."

"You're shameless," I said, shaking my head. "Anything to get out of school, right?"

She didn't answer. She sat roughly on the corner of my bed and stared at me.

"Don't shake the bed," I said, closing my eyes. "It hurts." I could feel her staring at my sling. "How's Mike doing?" I asked, just to say something.

She sighed. "He poops a lot."

"You must be so proud."

"So why did you ride into the bike racks? That was really stupid."

Olivia can be direct that way.

I opened one eye. "Amp stole my brake cables. No brakes."

"But that doesn't explain why you were going so fast."

"There was a flock of crows," I said quietly. "I rode through them."

"What is it with you and crows?" she whispered.

"They looked sinister," I said, using one of our vocabulary words. Olivia didn't notice.

"Did you know a group of crows is called a murder?" she told me.

"Seriously?" I shouted, wincing at the pain that shot up my arm.

"You rode through a murder."

Olivia knew more worthless information than anybody. If she said a bunch of crows was a called a murder, she was right.

"So why didn't you drag your feet on the ground?" she asked, changing the subject like a dancing prizefighter. "You could have slowed your bike down by dragging your feet on the ground."

"I don't know," I said, throwing my good arm up. "I didn't exactly have a lot of time to think."

"Olivia is right," Amp spoke up from somewhere near my desk.

"He dares to show his face?" I said.

"Council Note–"

Even without looking, I knew he had turned his back and was now speaking into the device he wore on his wrist.

"Please, not now, Amp," I pleaded. "You know those recorded reports for your bosses on planet Erde make me crazy."

He shushed me and continued.

**"Council Note: Earthlings do
not seem familiar with drag. Any
pressure distributed over a body
in motion exerts a force on that
moving body, the sum of which, of
course, reduces overall velocity, or
speed, in a given direction. Friction,
or resistance, as from dragging
your shoes on the ground while
you're riding your bike, dramatically
increases drag, reducing the overall speed of the body in motion."**

"You may as well be speaking Erdian," I said. "I have no idea what you're talking about."

"Seems pretty clear to me," Olivia said.

Amp was standing on my desk and, now that his report was concluded, began opening the SweeTarts wrapper. "The friction between your shoes and the ground would have absorbed a great deal of the kinetic energy."

"SAYS THE GUY WHO STOLE THE

BRAKES!" I shouted.

"There were a few things you could have done," Olivia said. "But you've never been very clear-thinking in emergencies."

"I agree with Olivia," Amp said, flicking Swee-Tarts into his mouth.

Here I was, wondering if I'd ever play another baseball game in my life, and they were busy criticizing me.

Sorry, but death by bike rack does not foster a lot creative ideas.

My eyes felt moist. I blinked away the start of some tears. I didn't want to cry in front of Olivia.

Instead, I cleared my throat and calmly said, "I think I need to rest."

On Being Lazy

"Oh my gosh, Olivia, get him off me!" I yelped. "He's gonna poop."

I'm not sure if I had drifted off to sleep for a moment or not, but Olivia had apparently taken Mike out and let him roam free.

"Chill, dude. They're just teeny-tiny hamster poops," Olivia said.

"They're still gross," I said. "I eat in this bed!"

Amp was about to finish off the last of the SweeTarts Olivia had brought him. Candy crumbs covered the crossword puzzle worksheet that was at the top of my stack of homework.

Amp wasn't just a sloppy eater; he was a lazy eater, too. His diet consisted mostly of SweeTarts and Ritz crackers. Just one of his many charms.

"While you were sleeping, I was thinking: you

could have slowed your bike down with a para-chute," Amp said.

I shot him a look. "Oh, you think I carry a parachute in my school backpack?"

"You should have had a backup system," Amp informed me. "It's called redundancy. If the first system fails, you have a backup at the ready to employ."

"Listen to this guy," I said to Olivia. "The alien who drilled the front of his spaceship into my bedroom wall is giving me a lecture about how to stop."

"You could have crashed your bike onto a bed," Amp added. "The kinetic energy of you and your bike would have been absorbed by the mattress."

"Good idea," Olivia said, high-threeing Amp.

"Really helpful, guys," I said. "I'll be sure to ask Principal Luntz to install a cozy set of bedroom furniture for the next time Amp steals my brakes."

"I didn't steal them," Amp said. "I borrowed them. Without asking."

Olivia laughed. "I like the way you think, Ampy."

"You guys are making my head hurt worse than my shoulder." I sighed.

"Council Note–"

"Oh, please stop!" I growled.

He ignored me and continued speaking into his wristband device.

**"Council Note: Boy Earthling
seems completely unaware of the
existence of kinetic energy, which
is merely the energy created as
a result of something moving. He
does, however, seem very familiar
with inertia, which is the tendency
to do nothing or to remain
unchanged. You should see him just
lying here!"**

"I have a headache," I said, staring at the ceiling.

"Do you want me to put Mikey on your head?" Olivia asked, dangling her pet above my head. "His little feet can massage your scalp."

"Yuck, no!" I said, pushing away her arm. "He'll poop in my hair."

Olivia was officially annoying me.

Amp was now walking in circles, enjoying the conversation. "Much of the energy from your crash could have been absorbed by something other than a bed. A pile of leaves. Soft dirt. Even bushes or ivy."

"Or I could have landed on Max Myers," I said. "He's kinda big and gooey."

"Exactly," Amp said, snapping his tiny fingers.

"I'm just joking," I said, rolling my eyes at his enthusiasm.

"We're just saying you can be a little slow in these situations," Olivia said.

"Yes, perhaps if you spent more time on your studies—"

"GET OUT!" I shouted. "BOTH OF YOU!" I yelled. "With friends like you, I should consider upgrading to enemies!"

"Zacky, I was just—" Olivia started, but I didn't let her finish.

"Just get away from me and leave me alone. The both of you!"

Just then, Mom knocked and opened the door.

I peeked out under my forearm in Amp's direction, but he had already made himself invisible.

"Sorry, Olivia, Zack needs to get some rest," Mom said sweetly. I was pretty sure she had heard me raise my voice.

"Okay," Olivia said awkwardly. The room was filled with uncomfortable silence. She left quietly without saying good-bye or "I'm sorry."

Egg on My Face?

I woke up feeling like I'd been beaten on the shoulder with an iron skillet.

It also felt like a dirty gopher had crawled into my mouth and died on my tongue.

My hair felt greasy and my T-shirt clung to my sweaty skin.

I seriously needed to stretch my muscles, take a hot bath, and brush my teeth for about an hour—and not necessarily in that order.

I turned my head to check if it was day or night, and that's when I saw my little brother's face inches from mine.

"AAAGH!" I gasped. "You never sneak up on a sleeping person like that, Taylor! I could have karate chopped you or something!"

"All you do is sleep," he said, waving his

hand in front of my face. "And oh my gosh, your breath . . ."

"What are you doing in here?" I said, suddenly realizing that he could have been poking around for the last hour, looking for Amp.

Despite being a total science nerd, Taylor had been unable to blow the lid off my little secret. He knew Olivia and I were up to something, but hadn't figured out that I was playing host to an intergalactic houseguest.

"Mom asked me to wake you up for dinner," he said. "She also said you're going to help me with my new Club Edison experiment."

"No way," I groaned. "I almost lost my arm! I don't want to do nerd experiments with my little brother. Why should I be punished?"

Taylor shrugged. "Don't blame me. It was Mom's idea. She said you're not playing baseball this weekend and that your sling will give you a chance to slow down and spend some quality time with a genius."

"Good grief," I said.

Just thinking of doing science experiments for fun gave me a brain cramp.

37

Taylor now held an egg up for me to see. "We'll be experimenting with these."

"Or we could make French toast," I said.

"We'll be doing an experiment about kinetic energy." Before I could stop him, Taylor held the egg above me as high as he could and dropped it. It hit my stomach and rolled off.

"Are you crazy?" I hollered, grabbing the egg.

"See, your belly is soft enough to absorb the energy in the falling egg. The impact didn't crack the shell."

"My belly isn't soft," I said, but I was reminded of what Amp had been saying earlier about a bed absorbing my energy. "Oh, I know all about Connecticut energy, smarty-pants."

Taylor stared at me. "Don't worry, Zack, I just need you to film the experiment for my YouTube channel," he said, patting my leg. "You don't actually have to think. Leave that up to your little bro. You'll just be, like . . . the assistant."

"I'm smarter than you think, twerp," I said, faking that I was throwing the egg at him. He ducked. I smiled. "Made you flinch."

He crossed to the door of my room, scanning

his eyes around the room as he did.

"Don't be so nosy," I said.

"Mom and Dad are down there waiting to eat, so hurry up . . . assistant."

I couldn't resist. I threw the egg for real this time—just as he closed the door behind him. It hit my bathrobe, which was hanging on the back and muffled the impact enough that it didn't break. That didn't happen until it hit the floor.

Egghead

After dinner, we sat there stuffed, staring at the mess on the table, too fat and satisfied to start cleaning up.

We had waffles. Weird, I know, but every two weeks or so, Dad cooks, and all he knows how to make are waffles, pancakes, or French toast. We're supposed to pretend like it's fun, but really it's just sticky.

"So, I hear you two have big plans for a new experiment on Taylor's YouTube channel?" Mom asked.

I rolled my eyes. I was using my napkin to wipe off the maple syrup I had accidentally dripped all over my sling. "I'm thinking of starting my own YouTube video channel."

"For what?" Taylor asked. "How-to-crash-your-bike videos?"

"Don't be a smart aleck, Taylor," Dad half said and half burped.

"It'll be nice for you two to spend some time together," Mom said. "Bonding."

"Do I have a choice? Usually you don't punish someone who nearly loses an arm, Mom."

"Listen to your mother," Dad mumbled, rubbing his belly with half-closed eyes.

"Maybe helping your brother record his experiments will inspire you," she said.

"To do what? Become a nerd?"

"Why'd I have that last waffle?" Dad groaned, his eyes closed in regret. "So, what's the experiment, sport?"

"Allow me to demonstrate," Taylor said, rushing to the refrigerator. He pulled out a Styrofoam container of jumbo eggs and a dish of green Jell-O. "Observe," he said. He placed the Jell-O on the table in front of his chair. He then stepped on his chair, plucked an egg out of the container, held his hand high above his head, and dropped the egg.

"Taylor!" Dad cried.

The egg sank into the wobbly green slime an inch or so, but it didn't break.

43

Taylor jumped up and down on his chair with excitement. "See, the Jell-O absorbs the egg's energy and it doesn't crack!"

"Be careful," Dad grumbled. "One broken arm at a time, please."

"It's not broken, it got dislocated," I said.

Instead of being angry, Mom clapped and laughed. "You are the cat's meow, Taylor," she exclaimed. "That's so neat! See, Zack—fun."

"Fun?" I said. "Seems like a dumb way to ruin a perfectly good bowl of Jell-O."

"Zack, your grades have been falling all year," Dad said. "You could stand to put in a little extra time on something educational."

"I don't need to be part of Taylor's lame experiments. I can do my own." I jumped up, snatched an egg from the container, and pulled about three feet of paper towels from the roll. I wrapped the towels around the egg and held the paper towel–wrapped egg high above my head. I gave my brother my watch-and-learn look, and dropped it.

The egg burst like a balloon. Some of the gooey yellow yolk and slimy egg white exploded from between the folds of the paper towel and splashed across my dad's face.

Dad's eyes popped open. "WHAT WAS THAT?!"

We all stared in complete silence.

"What am I going to do with you, Zack," Mom whispered, giving me her angry eyes.

"Dad, that was Zack displaying his ignorance of the basic laws of physics," Taylor said.

I looked across at Taylor. He stuck out his tongue at me.

I rolled my eyes. "Egghead," I said.

"Oh, I think you're the one with egg on his face," he said.

This made Dad chuckle. "I think that'd be me, actually," he said, and he and Taylor roared with laughter.

I didn't even get it.

I already knew this was going to be the worst weekend of my life.

Sleepyhead

Saturday morning I woke up in a panic.

My clock said 9:30 a.m. Baseball practice was at nine.

Then, as I reached to fling off my covers, a shooting pain in my shoulder reminded me I was damaged goods. My wing was broken. I would not fly today. I'd be grounded in the nest, playing with eggs.

I groaned.

I was sure Coach Lopez would forget about me. I would lose my place on my travel baseball team. My teammates would forget my name. They'd find another catcher—easy.

How did this happen to me?

One word: Amp!

My door popped open and Taylor stuck his head in. "Science waits for no man."

47

"Buzz off, egghead."

"Mom said. And you missed breakfast. And Olivia is on the phone for you."

"Tell her I will not be taking any of her calls today," I said. "And I'm not hungry. Now shut my door."

"Okay, cranky face," Taylor said. "But get up, I need a camera man."

I sat and burped loudly. Since Amp had entered my life, I hadn't slept well once. But since I hurt my shoulder, I was easily getting twelve to fourteen hours of sleep a night. My brain must be in shock.

Still in my sweaty T-shirt and pajama pants, I mummy-walked to the bathroom, then into Taylor's room. His floor was covered with several egg-holding contraptions in various states of completion. He was weighing little piles of parts on a tiny scale.

"Good morning, Igor," he said, not looking up. "Do you know how to shoot video on Mom's phone?"

"Of course I do," I snapped, despite the fact I had never done it before.

"How's this, Taylor?" my dad called from outside Taylor's window.

We both walked over and looked down to the

backyard below. My dad was standing on the grass in front of a giant, flat piece of wood that he had placed directly underneath Taylor's window. Dad was wearing his work gloves and holding a spray can.

"Look, I even spray-painted a big target on the board," Dad said.

"That's perfect, Dad!" Taylor shouted. "Isn't this the coolest, Zack?"

I imagined my baseball teammates forgetting about me at this very moment.

That's when I saw the balloon floating near Taylor's bed. It said HAPPY BIRTHDAY on it.

At that moment, I had a great science idea.

I snatched the scissors off Taylor's workbench, cut the balloon's string and caught the string as the balloon started to rise. I plucked an egg out of the Styrofoam container that was open on Taylor's bed and helped myself to the scotch tape dispenser on his desk. I quickly attached the egg to the string. With only one hand available, my work was a little messy, but sometimes science isn't pretty.

Taylor was still admiring Dad's spray-painted target out the window when I leaned out past

him. I held the egg in the hand of my good arm. I
let the balloon float up, aimed my egg, and let go.

"My balloon!" Taylor said.

In an instant I could tell the balloon wasn't big
enough to set the jumbo-sized egg down gently, as I had imagined it would. Instead, the egg
dropped like a boulder, pulling the helpless balloon behind it. The egg exploded dead center on
the target, the goop from the egg splashing onto
Dad's sneakers.

Dad's head snapped up at me like I was a mad-man. "Really, Zack? Again?" he yelled.

Now that the egg was scrambled, the balloon had no trouble lifting the tiny piece of taped shell still attached to the string. Taylor and I watched as it floated up over the roof and disappeared.

"Thanks a lot," Taylor hissed.

"It's just a lousy balloon," I said. I waved at Dad, who was giving me his angry face from the grass below. "Sorry, Dad. Learning can be messy."

He grumbled something to himself and walked off, shaking his head.

Taylor grunted and went back to preparing his egg contraptions on the floor. "Seriously, Zack, let me do the thinking, or this is going to be a very long and very messy weekend."

I walked past him without another word.

I had another idea—a better idea.

Egg Drop Derby

I pulled an old shoebox off the shelf in my closet. Among the trinkets and junk inside was a little plastic army guy with a parachute attached to his back. If I could untie the parachute strings tied to the little loop on the army guy's backpack, I could tape the parachute to an egg.

I smiled at my brilliance.

The parachute would set the egg down gently on the board and I could show Dad and Taylor my ideas were as good as any a brainy first grader could have.

At my desk, I had to use my teeth to work out the knot at the end of the parachute string. I was concentrating so hard on the task at hand I didn't see Amp approach.

"You must be very hungry," he said, suddenly

appearing from behind my cup of pencils and pens.

"Wha da you vant?" I said, holding the string between my teeth.

"You look like a beaver flossing his teeth," he said. "What are you doing to that poor green plastic man?"

"You're next," I said, giving him a look I hoped would convince him to disappear for a week.

"I saw your failed balloon experiment." He giggled. "That idea wasn't as bad as your usual ideas."

"I know," I said, feeling the top of the knot loosening and my patience fading.

"You simply miscalculated," he said, pointing at me. "If your balloon had been bigger, contained more helium inside, well, then, maybe you'd have something."

"I know," I said as the knot finally gave way and came unraveled.

Amp turned away and spoke into the device on his wrist.

"Council Note: The element helium is used here on Earth to make balloons float. Ha! Sort of a waste of a very useful gas. Although it is the second most abundant element in the universe after hydrogen, it's fairly rare here on Earth, and seems to be used

**only for making children's toys
float. Very curious indeed."**

"Do you do that just to bug me?" I asked. "If you do, it's working."

"Now you're going to try a parachute, aren't you?" Amp asked, ignoring my irritation. "Zack, I've been thinking."

"Oh no," I said.

"That switch you helped me with the other morning . . ."

"The one that made me late for school and ended up breaking my arm? That switch?"

"Dislocated, not broken. Yes, that switch. Anyway, my power booster is now working, thanks to you and that switch. That means I am very close to leaving."

"Really?" I said. "Huh, that's great, Amp. When can you go?"

"Well, that's just it. I may be able to get to Erde, but I wouldn't be able to stop. That crash into your bedroom wall would be nothing compared to how I'd hit planet Erde. I'd go splat, like a pancake."

"Bummer," I said. "Then fix your braking system. I'm kinda busy right now—"

"Which is why, Zack, this parachute idea has me so excited. See, it's all so simple: we could install a parachute like this one on my ship. The air on Erde is thicker than the air here on Earth. With the right entry angle into the Erde atmosphere, a parachute would work great."

"I'll let you know how this works," I said, standing.

"Well, that's just it," he said. "Let me take over this experiment. With my training, experience, and smarts, I think I could arrive at a solution much faster than with someone of your, your limited—"

My hand shot out and grabbed Amp. I cut him off mid-sentence. I had totally surprised him. Now he struggled to get free. His three-fingered hands pounded harmlessly on my fingers. He started to blink on and off in my sight, using his old disappearing trick in his panic, but it wasn't working.

"Actually, I don't need your help, Amp," I told him. "If I need a complete disaster, I'll call you. But this is my idea and I'll handle it on my own, without your meddling."

"Release me this instant," he demanded in his squeaky voice.

I was about to put him in my desk drawer when I saw Olivia's hamster ball sticking out from under my bed. What a great idea! Mike certainly wouldn't mind if Amp spent a few hours wandering around my room inside his plastic ball. The fact that it probably smelled like hamster poop wasn't my fault.

I placed Amp inside, and as quickly as I could, I replaced the cover and spun it back into place.

Now Amp put his hands on his hips and gave me his best Erdian stinkeye. "You wouldn't dare leave me in here, Zack. I am from an advanced civilization!"

"What? C'mon, you'll have a ball in there," I said, smirking.

"This isn't funny!" he cried. "It stinks in here."

I rolled the ball a few inches and Amp had to take a few steps so he didn't fall over. He looked so ridiculous I had to laugh. I rose to my feet, grabbed my toy parachute, and dashed to the door. Amp rolled after me, with a hilariously angry face. I closed the door before he got to me. I heard the plastic hamster ball bump off the other side of the door.

I smiled.

Maybe this weekend wasn't going to be so bad after all.

I headed down the hallway for a test that I was now thinking would put me back on top of the McGee Family Egg Drop Derby.

Runaway

I plucked an egg out of the carton on Taylor's bed. It took only a few seconds to yank out another piece of tape and attach the toy parachute to the egg.

"What are you doing?" Taylor asked suspiciously. "Is that a parachute?"

I ignored him and walked over to the window. Taylor pushed his way next to me. He pulled on my arm. I laughed. Science was even more fun than it looked!

"Stop wasting eggs," he cried.

I felt like one of those crazy scientist guys with the wild hair who always appear in Frankenstein movies. My laugh actually sounded a bit like a loony cackle.

"Dad, tell Zack to quit it."

My dad had just come through the backyard

gate. He was carrying a folding chair, which I think was for me to sit in while I filmed Taylor's egg drop.

"Watch this!" I called out.

I tossed the egg in the air. It went up as high as the roof, the parachute fluttering behind it. Then it began to fall. And like magic, the parachute popped opened beautifully, with the egg swinging comfortably underneath the parachute's umbrella.

"HA!" I shouted. "LOOK AT THAT, SUCKERS!"

Then something happened that had not occurred to me: the parachute started to drift. A sudden breeze blew my parachute off course.

"NO!" I cried as the parachute drifted away and across the backyard. The three of us stared wide-eyed as my helpless egg went on the ride of its life.

The parachute picked up speed as it continued to the other side of our backyard. I gasped as I saw it heading directly for our barbecue.

With a satisfying splat, the egg exploded against the barbecue as the parachute was blown out of sight.

Nobody moved.

"You really don't like eggs, do you?" Dad said.

My mom appeared behind us. She had her work laptop in one hand and the laundry in the other. "Look at my boys, working together."

"Zack has turned this into more of a food fight than a science experiment," Taylor complained.

I looked at the stack of Taylor's underwear that my mom was carrying.

"Wait, did you go into my room?" I blurted out.

"Yes, I did," Mom said, taken aback. "Why?"

"Did you close my door?" I said, grabbing her arm. I could tell by her face she hadn't.

I ran out of Taylor's room and looked down the hallway toward my door. I saw Amp emerge from my doorway and start running in the opposite direction, inside Mike's hamster ball. He was trying to escape!

Amp stopped for a moment, looked over his shoulder at me, then continued even faster down the hallway, the ball rotating around him. Without warning, he took a sharp left-hand turn toward the stairs.

I gasped. "No!"

"What was that thing!?!" Taylor whispered

from behind me.

I heard the plastic ball bouncing violently down the stairs. *THUMP! THUMP! THUMP!*

I stood frozen. Mike's ball bounced down the stairs. Then . . . after a few seconds of silence . . . I heard the ball hit the wooden floor. It bounced off the wall opposite the stairs and then . . . silence.

I turned and looked at Taylor and Mom. "Uh . . . nothing," I said.

"That was the loudest nothing I ever heard," Mom said.

I had just witnessed my third egg fall to its death. And now I was terrified that I'd find my alien houseguest splattered all over the inside of his plastic egg prison!

Before I could start moving, I heard the front door open downstairs. My dad made an odd noise. "Zack McGee! You need to get down here right now!" he hollered.

From the sound of his voice, I feared that my secret alien roommate had just become a whole lot less secret.

11

Doodles

I shot down the stairs so fast I don't actually remember my feet hitting the floor.

I hit the bottom step, slipped, bounced off the wall, and winced in pain.

My eyes wildly scanned the floor. There was no sign of Olivia's plastic hamster ball or its helpless blue prisoner.

"Zack, you need to see this!" Dad hollered from the front doorway.

I gulped. Even if Amp were able to make himself invisible, a ball rolling around under its own invisible power would surely cause a panic.

I tore off down the hallway. The sooner I started lying, the better.

My dad was leaning into the front doorway when I came shooting down the hallway. But he was smiling.

67

I hit the brakes and slipped again. My feet flew out from under me and I fell on my butt, like a wet bag of noodles. The fall hurt my shoulder so much I couldn't even scream.

"Here's the big joker now," Dad said to someone behind him and pushed the door open.

Standing behind him were Lexie Evans and Jade Bloom, two girls from my class. They'd brought me get-well cookies.

Lexie and Jade both stared at me in openmouthed shock.

Lexie cleared her throat. "Whoa, that looks like it hurt," Lexie said.

"No, I'm fine." I wheezed in pain, looking up at them through blurry eyes.

"Cool pajamas," Jade said quietly.

"What do you say, Zack?" Dad asked, looking down at me.

"I can't feel my butt," I groaned.

Both girls laughed. Dad helped me to my feet and took the plate of cookies into the kitchen for us.

"We heard you were in pretty bad shape," Lexie said, exchanging a look with Jade.

"Miss Martin told us you couldn't even get out of bed," Jade said.

"Oh, no," I said, distracted. I still had an escaped alien to capture. "I've been . . . pretty busy . . . actually."

A moment of silence passed.

"We hope you like snickerdoodles," Lexie said.

"What?" I said, looking back over my shoulder. "Oh, sure, I like doodles."

"You're acting so weird," Jade said with a giggle.

"Sorry," I said. "Pain pills."

"I heard you rode your bike into the bike rack because you were attacked by a flock of crows," Jade said.

"It's actually called a murder," I corrected. "A murder of crows."

"Some crows tried to murder you?" Lexie asked, shaking her head in confusion.

Rather than argue, I just said, "It wasn't an attack exactly. I got away. Look, thanks for popping over, but—"

"What is that?" Jade shouted, pointing behind me.

I spun and saw Olivia's hamster ball zigzag into the living room, seemingly on its own power—at least Amp had remembered to make himself invisible.

I spun around and tried to block the girls' view. "Oh, that's one of my brother's experiments that I—"

"Sorry, ladies," Dad interrupted, suddenly clapping his hand on my good shoulder. "Zack has to help his little brother with his science experiments for his YouTube channel."

"Zack?" Lexie said, raising her eyebrows. "You like science? Really? That's so cool."

"Oh, I'm into some pretty surprising stuff," I said awkwardly. I gave them a small, waist-high wave. "Thanks for the doodles."

"Bye?" they both said, puzzled.

Dad shut the door with a *click*. I stepped to the side so Dad turned away from the living room and the shock of his life.

"Nice of them to stop by, but enough foolishness," Dad said.

"But . . . ," I objected. I had to find Amp.

"No buts," Dad said. "Time to get back to work." He marched me out to the backyard and sat me down in the folding chair he'd set out. He

71

gave me Mom's smartphone, with the video camera function opened.

"Could I at least get dressed?" I asked.

Dad didn't respond.

"Some milk and a cookie?"

Dad glared.

"A bathroom break?" I asked.

He pointed at me and then up at Taylor's window. He gave me his firm no-nonsense look.

I decided not to mention then that there was an alien in our house, trapped in Olivia's plastic hamster ball, and that he was our only hope of stopping an interplanetary invasion before it happened. Somehow I didn't think he'd believe me.

How did my life get so out of control?

12

Egg Ball

I was so nervous about someone else finding Amp that I could hardly concentrate. Sure, he could make himself invisible if he saw you coming, but if you snuck up on him, he wouldn't know to go invisible—and then our little secret would get out. And, yes, he could erase your memory, but the chance of him turning my parents into mindless zombies was a risk I wasn't willing to take.

Twice I snuck in through the back door while Taylor was busy upstairs. On both occasions, my dad emerged out of nowhere before I had gotten two steps in.

"Don't test me," he said the last time.

"Okay!" I said. "But I've got problems of my own, you know!"

So there I sat. I'd film my brother doing a quick

introduction, then the egg drop, and, of course, the collision with the wooden board. Then I'd run over with the video still recording and—although Taylor had instructed me to wait for his arrival— see if there was still a whole, unbroken egg inside.

Taylor would join me out back and get excited about whatever adjustments he had to make. He'd scribble down some notes and then rush back upstairs.

There was a lot of downtime between egg drops. Science is slow. So, I decided to call Olivia with Mom's phone.

Her grandpa answered and put the phone down to get Olivia. But when the phone was picked up again, it wasn't Olivia, it was her grandpa. "Sorry, Zack," he said. "Olivia wants me to tell you she will not be taking any of your calls. She said you needed a taste of your own medicine. Sorry, fella."

"Oh," I said, embarrassed. "Thanks." I pushed the button to end the call.

My whole life was starting to fall apart. No friends. An alien on the loose. And Taylor was taking forever to make whatever adjustments he needed to.

"C'mon. I'll have a beard by the time you're done!" I shouted up at Taylor's window.

Suddenly, he poked his head out of *my* bedroom window!

"Some interesting things in here, Zack," he said. "What have you been up to?"

I jumped up. "Get outta my room!"

"If you leave that chair, I'm telling Dad you're sneaking away again," he said and disappeared back into my room.

"I'll scramble you!" I screamed at my now-empty window. "MOM! DAD! Taylor is snooping around my room!"

"Hey, Zack, look what I found downstairs," Taylor said, appearing in my window again, only this time with the plastic hamster ball in his hands!

I gasped.

He shook the ball in front of him. "How does this thing roll? What's in here? When I shake it, it feels like there's something inside, but I don't see anything. I'm going to open it."

I was so mad I could hardly speak. "DON'T TOUCH MY STUFF!"

I sprinted to the back door, threw it open, and shot down the hallway before my dad had time to cut me off.

"Hey, what did I tell you!" Dad boomed.

"I'm gonna pound that little snooper!" I responded.

"What's all this commotion?" Mom asked as I passed her at the top of the stairs.

I saw Taylor shoot out of my bedroom, across the hallway, and into the upstairs bathroom.

I grabbed the top towel off the folded stack she was holding and flung it down the hall with my good arm, right at the closing bathroom door.

I could see Taylor inside, rushing to shut the door and lock me out. Luckily, the towel I had thrown wedged itself between the door and the jamb, preventing Taylor from shutting it.

I slammed my shoulder into the door. My left shoulder. The one in a sling.

With a squeal of pain, I stumbled backward and fell to the carpet.

Then I think I fainted.

13

Ring-a-Ding

I woke up to bells ringing.

My parents and Taylor were standing over me. Everything sounded far away and looked out of focus.

And the bells didn't stop.

"You could have killed him!" Dad thundered at Taylor.

"Me?" Taylor said. "I was just going to the bathroom when he ran into the door!"

"He said you were snooping," Mom said. "Were you?"

"He stole my ball!" I croaked, pointing to the ball held under Taylor's arm. "He's a thief!"

"That's a lie," Taylor said. "This ball rolled right past me downstairs."

I kept hearing bells ringing. Was real life like

cartoons? When you get knocked out, you hear bells ringing?

"Who is at the door?" Dad hollered in frustration.

"It better be important," Mom said, throwing her arms up.

"I'll get it," Taylor said, turning to go, the ball still under his arm.

"Oh, no, you don't," I said and slapped the ball out from under his arm.

The ball bounced off the wall and landed next to me. The bouncing must have thrown off Amp's focus because he suddenly appeared stumbling around inside the ball.

I had no choice. I threw my body over the ball.

"What was that?" Taylor shouted.

"What was what?" Dad snapped.

"It's like a fat blue hamster . . . or something."

"Don't be ridiculous," Dad said.

"This ball is none of your business!" I shouted.

"Zack!" Olivia screamed.

Everyone stopped and turned to see Olivia standing at the top of the stairs looking out of breath and bug-eyed. "I let myself in."

"What's in that ball? How does it roll by itself?" Taylor asked her.

Olivia walked past him and kneeled down next to me. She grabbed the plastic ball from me and placed it inside a brown paper bag, the kind you get from the grocery store.

"It's just a trick ball," she said.

She pulled the ball back out of the bag as she removed the circular door.

"Olivia, don't," I cried.

"It's okay, Zack," she said calmly. "It's just a trick."

She walked over to show my dad and Taylor. Taylor stuffed his hand into the ball and felt around inside. "Okay, but how does it roll around on its own?"

"A real magician never reveals her secrets," she said. "I *will* tell you that this illusion is called 'The Invisible Hamster.'"

"How clever," Mom said, impressed.

While they were distracted, I peeked into the paper bag. And sure enough, there was Amp, on the bottom of the bag, looking dazed and confused. Olivia had secretly dumped him out!

Olivia had many interests, and one of them was

magic. I had to admit, that was a skill that came in handy more often than you'd imagine. Her other talents—like being able to bake banana bread, make realistic animal noises, dance like a robot, and speak in weird accents—had not proven to be as useful.

Yet.

Olivia gave me another smile and she picked up the "empty" bag. "Now if you'll excuse me, I have to go practice my magic."

With that, she gently placed the ball back in the bag and we all watched her walk down the hallway and descend the stairs.

Mom let out a thunderous sigh. "Zack, I'm sure this is a good time for another pain pill."

"No more nonsense for the rest of the day," Dad said. He picked up his cell phone, which I had dropped, and he and Mom headed downstairs, leaving Taylor and me in the hallway.

"I don't know what you two are up to," Taylor said, "but I'll figure it out sooner or later."

"I can't wait," I said, rubbing my shoulder. I thought of Amp's spaceship and how close we were to sending him back home, which would save Earth from an Erdian invasion. "Look, Taylor, I think I was onto something with that parachute. What do you say we take another shot at that idea, for science's sake?"

Taylor studied my face to see if I was making fun of him. "Seriously?" he asked. "Did the bathroom door damage your brain or something?"

I smiled. "Maybe. But let's just say I'm curious on behalf of a friend of mine."

This seemed to satisfy him. He waited for me to reveal more, but I just stared back. He sighed. "Okay. I've built some bigger parachutes that you may want to see. Or your friend may want to see," he said, making air quotes with his fingers on the word "friend."

And with that, I spent the next hour getting schooled by my bossy little brother in the science of parachute design, operation, and maintenance.

One thing was for sure: Amp owed me big time.

14

Couching Concerns

"**O**kay, guys, this is crazy. You two need to kiss and make up. Or shake hands. Or whatever."

Olivia sat between Amp and me. We were all on the old, dusty couch in her grandpa's garage. It was our regular hangout, away from the prying eyes of Taylor and my parents. Amp sat on the arm at the other end of the couch and glared at me, shaking his head. I kept rolling my eyes at him.

"Please, you two, it all worked out in the end, right?" Olivia said.

"I could have been killed in that floofy hamster ball." Amp simmered.

"I could have been killed on that metal bike rack," I said back.

Olivia had in her lap the plate of cookies Lexie and Jade had brought me.

"How good was I, huh?" Olivia continued, now talking with her mouth full of snickerdoodles. "I used that paper bag as my blind; that's what a magician calls something that blocks the view of the audience. Fooled the whole McGee family. . . ."

"I wasn't fooled," I said.

"I wouldn't know," Amp said. "At the time, my brain was scrambled like an egg, thanks to Zack."

"I bet my big toe is bigger than your brain."

"Sheesh, I'm stuck between Grumpy and Grumpier," Olivia said, picking up her fifth cookie.

Yes, I was counting. They were my cookies, after all.

"How did you know we were in trouble, anyway?" I asked.

"Duh!" Olivia said. "I heard you screaming in your backyard about Taylor going into your room. The whole neighborhood probably heard you."

"I wasn't that loud."

She pulled Mike out of her sweatshirt pocket and began feeding him cookie crumbs while he wandered around on her thigh.

That was the last straw. I grabbed a cookie

from the plate and bit off half.

"Listen, I know you guys are steamed at each other. I get that. But at least Amp is safe. Our secret is still a secret. The world isn't turned upside down. No harm, no foul. Right?"

"I'll take a cookie," Amp said quietly.

"Really?" Olivia said. "Wow, Amp, expanding your diet! Now I know anything is possible."

She handed him a cookie and he nibbled on the edge of it without enthusiasm.

Without saying it, I was pretty sure this was Amp's way of saying sorry. He was trying to patch things up; he just wasn't able to apologize properly.

"You did look funny running around in that ball," I said.

"I wish I could have seen you flying over your handlebars," Amp said.

We looked at each other. I had to smile. It was hard to be angry with a blue guy no bigger than Pop-Tart.

"I guess we're even," I said, taking a second cookie.

"See, look at how mature you guys are. Two civilizations coming together over snickerdoodles.

They should fly me to the Middle East."

"Perhaps I can hear something about these parachutes you and your brother were experimenting with," Amp said, putting down the cookie and brushing the cookie dust off his fingers.

"Perhaps you're thinking of something like this." I reached behind me and pulled out a large silk parachute I had borrowed from Taylor—borrowed without asking, of course. But I'm sure that once I explained to Taylor that his missing parachute prevented two civilizations from fighting with each other, he would understand.

Olivia whistled. "Wow, that looks professional."

Amp crossed the couch for a closer look. He nodded as he ran the parachute through his little blue fingers and studied the fabric intently. "Light. Strong. Compact. It's perfect. I must say, I'm impressed."

"This parachute should be perfect for the size and weight of your spaceship."

Amp seemed relieved. "Well done, Zack McGee. We're closer than ever to sending me home."

"You owe me, short stuff," I said.

"Nice work, Zacky," Olivia said, punching me lightly on the leg. "Now, you two, can we sit back, relax, and enjoy these cookies that Zack's girl-friend made?"

"Girlfriend?! She's not my girlfriend!"

"Really? These cookies were made with love, for sure."

This made us all laugh. Even Mike, but that may have been my imagination again.

THE END

Try It Yourself:
The De-Eggcelerator

As Zack finds out, as much fun as it is to go fast, it's not nearly as fun if you can't slow down! You probably know this, too, if you've ever crashed your bike, fallen down some stairs, run into a tree while playing in the yard, or even tumbled off of a slide at the playground that was faster than you expected.

No matter what you're doing, whether it's biking, running, driving, or even flying in an airplane, there are really only two ways to slow down: the fast way (we call that crashing) and the slow way (much preferred). We use brakes of all different types in order to slow down the slow way and avoid crashing.

By why do we slow down sometimes and crash others? Imagine jumping off the top of the slide. You know not to do that, right? You could get hurt really bad! But why would it hurt? One way to think about it is that your legs (the brakes, in this case) don't slow you down enough to cushion your impact after jumping off something that tall. You need better brakes.

But what if, instead of jumping off a jungle gym, you slide down the fire pole. It's the same distance and the same direction. Instead you can reach the bottom without getting hurt. That's because your hands act like brakes. They slow you down as you go!

This is the idea we're going to employ in our own egg drop experiment. But we're going to do it a little differently. We're going to give that egg a set of brakes to slow it down. If we design it right, we can stop the egg the slow way so that it doesn't crack on impact.

Add brakes to avoid breaks!

For this experiment, you'll need:

- A yardstick, preferably the cheap kind made of wood
- A pair of pliers (not the needle-nosed kind)
- A few feet of string
- A drinking straw
- Strong tape
- A few rubber bands
- Some paperclips or wire
- A plastic cup
- Cardboard (a small-ish piece)
- A small tarp to help contain the mess if the egg breaks
- MOST IMPORTANT: An adult to help

1. Cut the piece of cardboard into a strip that's about an inch wide and two inches long. Fold it in half, and tape it onto the jaws of the pliers (the grabby part) to create a closed loop that can open and close a little bit. Make sure the tape is secure. The cardboard will be pinched by the pliers against the yardstick, creating brake pads that will slow the egg as it slides down the yardstick.

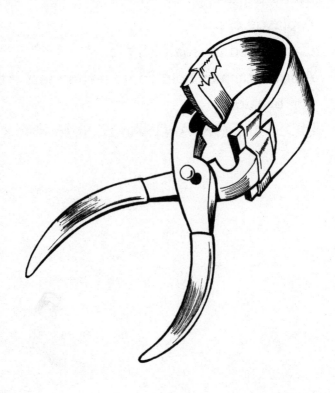

2. Cut two pieces off the drinking straw, each about 1" long. Tape one piece to each end of the yardstick, both on the same edge. This will create the guide that helps make sure the egg drop brake system falls straight down.

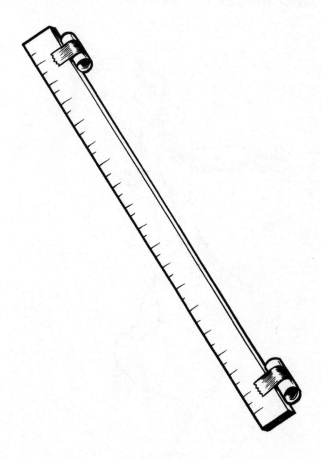

3. Carefully poke a small hole in the cup below its rim. Thread the wire (could be a big paperclip) through the hole, and loop the end around the pivot of the pliers so that the cup can securely hang beneath the pliers. Give the wire a few twists around itself to help make sure it doesn't fall off either the pliers or the cup.

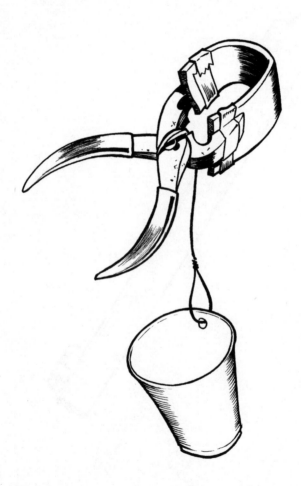

4. Open the pliers (spreading the closed loop of the jaws + cardboard) and loop the brake pads over the yardstick. Put a rubber band around the handles of the pliers, pulling them together. This should clamp the cardboard against the yardstick with a bit of a squeeze. Pick up the yardstick—do the pliers and cup hang in place on their own? If not, add another rubber band.

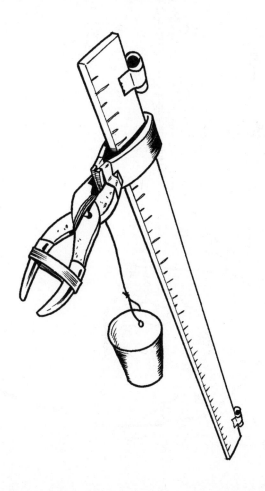

5. Put down a tarp that covers as much area as you can around the experiment site, in case your egg doesn't slow down enough and breaks!

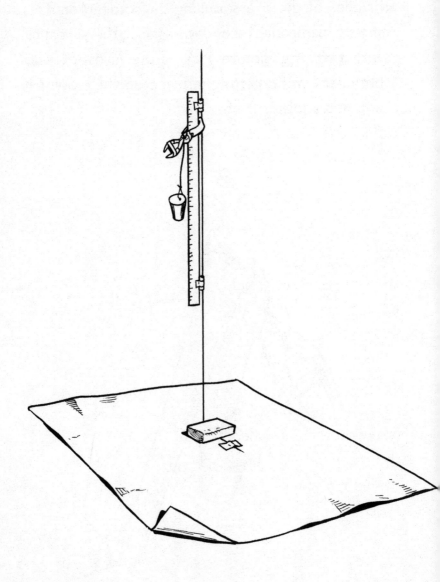

6. Set up the guide string vertically by tying it to something a few feet off the ground. This might be the top of a table, a staircase banister, or even an upper hinge of a door in the house. Thread the string through the drinking straw guides on your yardstick, and tape the bottom end of the string to the tarp. Blue masking tape is a kind of tape that won't leave a residue.

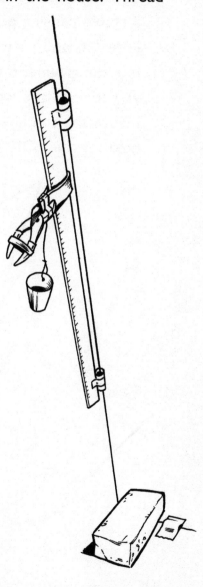

Make the string a little bit tight so that the yardstick can slide up and down while the string guides it vertically.

If the string pulls the tarp up when you add tension, put something heavy on the end where the tape is. A brick should work well.

7. Pretest! Put something in the cup that weighs about as much as an egg. A rock might do, or a small beanbag. Position the pliers up at the top of the yardstick, and allow them to settle into a stable hanging position. Lift up the yardstick a little bit, and then drop it. When the yardstick hits the ground, the pliers should slide down the yardstick a little way, hopefully coming to a stop before the cup hits the ground, too. If everything held together OK, it's time for the real test!

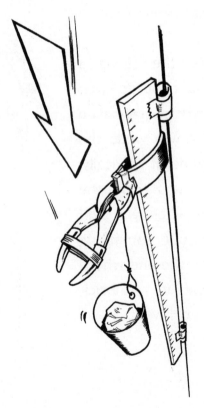

8. Slide the pliers back to the top, and let them hang naturally with the cup below. Place the egg into the cup. Pick up the yardstick to your chosen height, cross your fingers, put on your safety glasses, and give a countdown. It's eggsperimentation time! *SPLAT*.

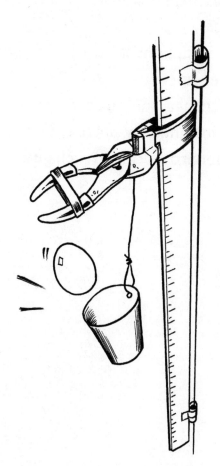

Questions to Ask

- Did the egg break?
- How far down the yardstick did the egg slide before it came to a stop?
- What happens when I add more rubber bands?
- What happens if I drop the yardstick from higher up?
- If I change the surface of the brake pads (for instance, by putting duct tape over the cardboard), does that change anything?

Troubleshooting

- **My egg hits the ground every time!**
  Try adding more rubber bands. If everything is set up right, but the egg still hits the ground, it might be that you need to squeeze harder on the brakes. You could also try dropping the yardstick from a lower height to begin with.

- **My egg keeps coming out of the cup!**
  You could add some tape to keep it in the cup. This experiment is designed to show the power of controlled deceleration in just one direction—downward. So if things are tippy and the egg is falling out, it's going to be harder to make good observations in the one direction you're interested in. Go ahead and do what's needed to keep it in place.

- **The yardstick comes off the string guides!**
  Add more tape.

More...

This is an experimental setup that can allow you to learn a lot of different things about what's going on! That's because it's relatively easy to repeat exactly the same conditions multiple times, allowing you to change small things and then very accurately record the differences. Try out lots of different combinations—different drop heights, different amounts of squeeze on the pads (adding or subtracting rubber bands), changing the brake pad material, and even seeing if you can slow down *two* eggs instead of one. What kinds of things do you observe with each change? What does that tell you about other things that you want to slow down, like a car, or a bus, or a bike, or yourself going down a slide or fire pole?

Have fun, and try not to make too big of a mess!

OHM vs. AMP

My Secret Roommate

When a pint-size alien from outer space crash-lands his spaceship on your bed during the middle of the night, your life can get pretty messed up.

You can never go back to the way it was.

My little blue alien and I argued constantly for two straight months as we tried to repair his junky ship. We fought like two crabs in a bucket.

Then we ran out of steam.

And we learned to get along.

I guess you can get used to most things that

1

at first seem to be the absolute ruin of your life, like summer school, tuna fish, and spelling quizzes.

I had grown comfortable with Amp, and he had gotten used to me.

The fact that Amp wasn't much bigger than a stick of butter helped me keep him a secret from my parents and little brother. He also had an invisibility trick that had come in handy more than once and the ability to erase people's short-term memory.

The only other person on Earth who knew about Amp was my best friend and next-door neighbor, Olivia. And she had gotten so used to Amp that it was a minor miracle she hadn't blurted out some funny story about him to my parents.

As the ambassador of the human race, I think I had done a pretty spectacular job. My cat hadn't eaten Amp, I hadn't stepped on him, and most important of all, I'd convinced him that attacking our planet was a bad idea.

See, Amp is the lead scout for the planet Erde. The Erdians are planning on taking over

Earth, but because of me, Amp understood that attacking this planet was a major mistake. Compared to the average Erdian, we were simply too big to be defeated.

So as we made slow progress in repairing his ship, the *Dingle*, we became friends—if it's possible for a human to be friends with a hairless, three-fingered, Smurf-colored alien no bigger than a ham sandwich.

But now the time was fast approaching to get Amp back home to cancel the Erdian invasion. The future of Earth and Erde depended on us. We both knew it, but we didn't talk about it much.

Mostly, we spent our time eating junk food and watching scary movies on my mom's laptop.

Amp was crazy for horror movies, the old black-and-white kind. *Dracula. Frankenstein. The Wolf Man. Creature from the Black Lagoon.* We were working our way through a deluxe set of twenty-four classic horror movies on DVD that I had borrowed from Olivia's grandpa.

One night, Amp and I were up late—as usual—enjoying SweeTarts and Ritz Crackers

3

while watching *The Mummy* (starring Boris Karl-off), when our cozy little situation got crazy.

As is often the case, it all started with alarm bells.

Sound the Alarm

"**H**ey, what's that noise?"

"Eh?" Amp grunted absent-mindedly. He was lying on his side next to the track pad on my mom's laptop, rubbing his stuffed belly, totally absorbed in the movie.

I was sitting cross-legged on my bed with the computer in front of me.

"Hey," I said, gently poking the back of his head with my pinky finger. "Can you hear that?"

"I can hear you interrupting the movie," he said. "Now shush."

"Seriously," I said, poking his shoulder now.

"Knock it off, Zack," he said, shrugging his poked shoulder.

"C'mon, Amp, listen."

"Quiet!" he said, waving his hand at me. "The

mummy is coming. I love this part!"

I slapped the space bar and paused the movie.

"What are you—?"

"Can you hear it now?"

We both listened in the silence. It was a far-away tinkling, buzzing sound. Or beeping. It wasn't the kind of sound I had ever heard before.

"That sounds pretty dang alien to me," I whispered.

He jumped to his feet and held up his hands to silence me as he strained to hear the noise.

"Oh, that's not good," he said in his strange, high-pitched voice.

"What exactly do you mean by 'not good'?"

"Does it mean more than one thing?" he asked.

"Amp, what's happening?"

He began looking around in a panic. His face turned a paler shade of blue.

"Is that sound coming from you? Are you going to explode or something?"

He shot me a look. "Don't be ridiculous. I don't beep. Or explode."

"At first I thought you were farting," I

half-joked, but it wasn't funny. The far-off beeping alarm grew louder.

"It's an Erdian alarm."

"Seriously?" I yelped, jumping off my bed. I dropped down to the floor and looked under the bed. I looked in my laundry basket. I opened all the drawers of my desk as fast as I could, but I seemed to get no closer to the sound. I noticed he was still standing on the laptop. "Are you just going to stand there?" I snapped.

"You can search faster than me," he said.

"Is the thing I'm looking for going to blow up in my face when I find it?!"

"Why do you always assume things are going to blow up?"

"That's the kind of noise things that blow up make!"

"Try the window," he said, pointing urgently.

I pulled up my window and looked out to the dark backyard. "Crickets," I said. "Only crickets outside. No alarm."

When I turned back around Amp was staring at the closet with a horrified expression on his face. We kept his spaceship in my closet!

Amp and I exchanged a glance, and I knew it was his ship.

I tiptoed over to my closet door, opened it slowly, and gently pulled the wool blanket off his spaceship. The alarm become louder as it fell away. I saw a small purple light blinking on the side of his football-size ship.

My mind spun. "Do you need to change the oil or something?"

Amp appeared next to my foot. He grabbed the ample skin of his belly and began to nervously knead it in his hands like bread dough. "That is a proximity alarm," Amp said in a trembly, tight voice.

"That's terrible," I whispered, staring at the blinking light. "What exactly does *proximity* mean?"

"It means someone is coming," he said.

Party Crasher

"What do you mean, somebody is coming?" I asked.

Amp pulled on his antennas. "What do you think I mean? I mean what it sounds like I mean!"

I picked him up and held him just inches from my nose. "Don't get tricky, Short Pants."

"I don't wear pants! You know that."

"Don't get snarky, either. Just tell me what's happening."

He released his antennas, closed his eyes, and pulled down his lower lip. "I don't know."

"They're attacking Earth, aren't they?" I yelped, shaking him.

"Who is?"

"Your creepy Erdian friends! They're arriving on Earth right now. The invasion is beginning, and

I never warned anybody!"

"Whoa, whoa, whoa!" he wheezed, struggling in my grip. "Not so fast."

"Was this whole thing a trick? Were you just stalling? Faking me out about your broken ship until your army of blue buddies arrived?"

He pushed on my fingers. "You're squeezing me too tight," he gasped. "My head is going to pop!"

"Sorry," I said and opened up my hand. He took several deep breaths and began to pace in circles on my palm, just inches from my face.

"That, Zack, is not an invasion alarm," he said, pointing at his ship. "Invasion alarms are yellow."

"Why yellow?"

"It would take too long to explain that," he said, waving off my question. "The point is that alarm just means that someone is coming."

"Someone? Or a million Erdian someones?"

He stared at the buzzing, flashing light and it stopped suddenly. He looked back at me. "They're probably trying to find me. Like a rescue mission of some kind. But because my ship is damaged, they'll never actually find me. The odds are a million to one."

I looked at him skeptically. "Who would they send? Your mom?"

"Why on Erde would they send my mother? That would make no sense. Let's just hope it's not my—"

Amp was interrupted by a thunderous whooshing sound coming from my window.

"Maybe the attack really is beginning!" I squealed.

I dropped Amp like a hot potato, jumped out of the closet, scrambled to my desk, and pressed my face to the window screen. I squinted as a fiery light lit up the backyard.

"Uh-oh," Amp gasped from somewhere behind me.

A spaceship just like Amp's was flying in circles twenty feet off the ground in our backyard. The shower of orange-and-white sparks spraying out of the spaceship made it look like the Fourth of July had come to my backyard.

Without warning, it turned sharply, like it had bounced off an invisible wall.

"Ooohhhhh nooooooo . . ."

I dove to the carpet just as the thing exploded through my window screen.